Two Little Chicks Go to School

by Valeri Gorbachev

NorthSouth
New York / London

One fine day, Mother Hen took her two little chicks to school for the very first time.

The little chicks were a little scared.

"Don't worry," said Mother Hen as she waved good-bye. "I'm sure you will like it here."

"Hello," said Mrs. Heron, the teacher. "Welcome to my class."

"We're scared," said the chicks. "We don't know anyone."

"Don't worry," said Mrs. Heron. "I'm sure you will make friends quickly."

During playtime all the chicks could think about was making friends. Beaver is very big, they thought. It would be good to have him as a friend. So they walked up to Beaver and said hello.

"*Shhhhhhh*," said Beaver. "I'm trying to build this tower."

During story time the chicks sat next to Rabbit. Rabbit looks friendly, they thought. She would be a good friend. So they turned to Rabbit and said hello.

"*Shhhhhh*," said Rabbit. "I'm listening to the story."

During music time the chicks stood next to Frog. Frog is little just like us, they thought. Maybe he would be our friend. So they turned to Frog and said hello.

"*Shhhhhhh,*" said Frog. "I'm trying to sing."

During snack time the two little chicks sat all by themselves. No one wants to be friends with us, they thought.

"How do you like school?" asked
Mrs. Heron.

"We can't make any friends,"
said the two little chicks sadly.

"Just wait," said Mrs. Heron.
"I have a feeling you will make
friends soon."

After everyone cleaned up, it was time to go outside.

"Come along," said Mrs. Heron. "We'll go to the meadow."

The whole class cheered.

On the way, everyone crossed a little stream. Everyone, that is, except the two little chicks.

"What's wrong?" asked Mrs. Heron.

"We're too little," said the chicks. "We might fall off the rocks—and we can't swim."

"Don't be silly," said Beaver. "The water isn't very deep. You can do it."

"No we can't," said the chicks. "We're just little chicks."

"I could build a bridge over the water," said Beaver.

"I could carry them across,"
said Rabbit.

"I could teach them how to swim,"
said Frog

"Thank you all," said Mrs. Heron. "But I have a better idea. Why don't you hold hands with the chicks and help them over the rocks?"

So they all held hands and slowly crossed the stream.

"We did it!" cried the two little chicks. "Thank you for helping us."

The two little chicks had a wonderful time playing in the meadow with their new friends. And on the way back to school, they scampered across the rocks all by themselves.

"Hooray for the two little chicks!" everyone shouted.

After school Mother Hen was
waiting. "Goodness," she said
as the little chicks ran down the
stairs. "You both look very happy."

"We *like* school," said the two
little chicks. "We made lots of
friends!"